ZAC
Multi~coloured
Spidajig

Kathleen Crawford

Illustrated by Gunvor Edwards

Scripture Union
130 City Road, London EC1V 2NJ

By the same author

Christopher's Band
The Grumpy Princess

First published 1993

ISBN 0 86201 844 7

British Library Cataloguing-in-Publication Data.
A catalogue for this book is available from the British
Library.

Phototypeset by Intype, London

Printed and bound in Great Britain by Cox and Wyman
Ltd, Reading

Contents

Zac and the multi-coloured Spidajig   5

Just Ted   12

God's World   19

When Dad lost his voice   23

The Wind   29

Sam and the hole in the road   30

Mrs McMuddle goes shopping   38

What a nuisance!   46

The Circus   52

Shussh!   54

Scallywag gets jealous   61

One of those days!   68

Hands   75

Oranges, ribbons and candles   76

Daniel's favourite colour   84

Emma and the tambourine   90

For
Sarah Clark, Billy Daykin, and Jonathan Douglas

Zac and the multi-coloured Spidajig

One morning when Zac was at playgroup he peered into the boxes where all the empty cartons, wool, shiny paper and bits and pieces for making models were kept.

'Hmmm, what shall I make today?' he wondered.

He put both hands into one of the big cardboard boxes and rummaged around to see what he could find. After all, the most interesting things are usually underneath everything else!

So Zac rummaged and rummaged until he found a plastic cup, some blue crinkly paper, and some strips of coloured paper that were left over from making paper chains at Christmas. He dipped a spreader into the pot of thick white glue and put blobs of glue on top of the plastic cup . . . and on his yellow jumper . . . and on his dungarees.

'I think you need to put on an apron before you do any more sticking,' said Mrs Robinson, and she helped Zac to find one and fasten it.

Zac took a handful of blue crinkly paper and stuck it on top of the cup.

'Blue hair,' said Mrs Robinson. 'That's interesting.'

'Yes,' said Zac, 'I'm making a really interesting sort of monster.'

Mrs Robinson walked away to look after one of the other children and Zac looked in the box to see what he could find to make some eyes. He saw some milk bottle tops and circles of bright pink paper, so he took two of each.

'Just what I need,' he thought and stuck them onto the cup too.

Very carefully he cut out a smiling mouth from some red shiny paper. It was rather a wobbly smiling mouth but Zac did not mind. He found another circle of bright pink paper and stuck that onto the cup to make a nose. Mrs Robinson came back. 'What a scary monster!' she said.

'He's actually a very friendly monster,' Zac told her. 'Look, he's smiling.'

'So he is,' agreed Mrs Robinson, 'but I still don't think I'd like to meet him on a dark night!'

She showed Zac how he could fold the strips of paper to make legs for his monster. Zac wanted to make it into a sort of spider but he was not sure how many legs a spider had. He thought it might be six or even eight so he decided to make his spider different and give it seven legs instead – all different colours. Then he put it on a table for the glue to dry.

'Aren't you going to put your name on him?' asked Mrs Robinson.

'No,' said Zac, 'there's only one monster like mine.'

'Look what I've made,' Zac said to Mum as she arrived to collect him at lunchtime.

'Very good,' said Mum. 'Where are you going to keep it? It looks a bit scary to me.'

'Of course it's not,' laughed Zac. 'He's really a very friendly sort of monster.'

'If we thread some elastic through the top part, you could hang it up in your bedroom,' suggested Mum.

Zac thought that was a very good idea.

'Look what I've made,' said Zac, rushing up to Dad as soon as he came home from work. He waved the spider in front of him and let it bounce up and down on the elastic.

'Goodness,' said Dad, pretending to be frightened. 'A monster with blue hair – from outer space, is it?'

'Of course not,' laughed Zac. 'Guess again.'

'Then it's most definitely a multi-coloured thingummyjig,' said Dad.

Zac was not sure what one of those was.

'Of course it's not,' he said. 'It's a spider.'

'It can't be,' said Dad. 'I've never seen a spider with blue hair before – and it's only got seven legs. I think spiders have eight legs.'

'Oh,' said Zac, 'well perhaps this one has had an accident.'

'Maybe,' smiled Dad. 'I know what, as it looks quite like a spider and its legs are all different colours why don't you call it a multi-coloured spidajig – Spidajig for short?'

Zac thought that was a very good name for his monster.

Dad fastened the end of the elastic to the curtain rail in Zac's bedroom so that Spidajig could bounce up and down as much as he liked and he would be there when Zac woke up in the morning. Dad gave Zac a big hug and they asked God to look after their family during the night and keep them safe. Zac sat his favourite teddy on his pillow, as he always did, and lay in bed happily thinking about all the things he had done at playgroup. He looked at Spidajig bouncing up and down on the piece of elastic.

'Goodnight, Spidajig,' he said sleepily. 'See you in the morning.'

Spidajig looked at Zac with a rather wobbly but happy smile. Zac closed his eyes and was soon fast asleep.

In the middle of the night, Zac woke up suddenly. He could hear scratching and squealing noises outside. He grabbed Teddy and squeezed him really tightly. Zac felt very frightened. He opened his eyes slowly – everywhere seemed dark even though Dad had left the door open slightly. Zac could hear a strange rustling noise in the garden and the yellow and white striped curtains were flapping about in front of his bedroom window.

Then he saw a pair of big shiny eyes staring at him in the darkness and there was a black shape moving up and down the wall. Zac did not like it at all. By this time he was very, very scared and the squealing noises outside were getting louder. Zac grabbed Teddy and ran along the landing into his mum and dad's room as fast as he could.

'Whatever's the matter?' asked Dad.

'Please come quickly,' said Zac, 'I'm frightened.'

And still holding tightly to Teddy with one hand and squeezing one of Dad's hands with the other, Zac went as far as his bedroom door.

'Look,' he said, 'there are monsters in my bedroom. One of them has got big shiny eyes and there is another one climbing up and down the wall.'

Dad looked. Zac stood behind him and held tightly onto Dad's pyjamas. Dad switched the light on. 'I can't see any monsters in here,' he said.

Zac put his head slowly round the door. The monsters had disappeared. All he could see was Spidajig smiling in the window. Dad hugged Zac tightly and switched off the light again. 'Is this what you saw?' he asked. Zac looked and nodded.

Spidajig's eyes were shining and glowing in the dark and there was a shadow on the wall which moved as Spidajig moved in the breeze. Dad took Spidajig down from the curtain rail and sat him on the toybox.

'There were funny noises too,' said Zac. 'Spidajig didn't make those.'

'It was probably the ginger and white cat from next door fighting with one of his friends on the garden wall,' Dad told him. 'Or perhaps you heard the wind blowing through the leaves on our cherry tree, or an owl hooting.'

'I was really frightened,' said Zac. 'It was horrible.'

'Lots of people are frightened at night,' said Dad. 'When it's dark and quiet, everything seems so different. But all you have to do to make the darkness go away is to put a light on. If you're scared you only have to tell us and you know we'll always come and look after you.'

Zac began to feel much happier and snuggled back into his bed. Dad closed the bedroom window. 'It won't be so noisy now,' he said, 'and your curtains won't flap in the breeze.'

He looked at Zac. 'Quick, there's a rabbit on that wall,' he said.

'Don't be silly,' laughed Zac. 'Of course there isn't.'

But he looked – just in case – and sure enough there was a rabbit with floppy ears and a twitching nose. Then the shape changed into a bird and then into a butterfly which began to fly across the wall.

'It's a trick, isn't it?' laughed Zac as he saw Dad's hands move. 'Will you show me how to do that? Please?'

'Yes,' answered Dad, 'but not now.' He yawned. 'I think we both need some sleep.'

Dad tucked Zac into bed again, gave him a hug and left the light on so that he was not frightened.

Next time he went to playgroup, Zac told Mrs Robinson all about Spidajig and how his eyes had shone and glowed in the dark.

'I told you I wouldn't want to meet him on a dark night,' she laughed.

'Are *you* frightened of the dark?' Zac asked.

'Sometimes,' said Mrs Robinson.

'I am,' said Zac.

Mrs Robinson went to the cupboard where all the coloured paper was kept. 'I've got an idea,' she told Zac, and she took a piece of black paper and cut out some star shapes. She gave him a piece of bright yellow tissue paper.

'Put some glue round the edges,' she told him, 'and then put this piece of paper on top so that it covers all the star-shaped holes.'

Zac got a spreader and dipped it into the pot of thick white glue. But this time he did not drip blobs of glue on his jumper and dungarees because he had remembered to put an apron on first.

'Can I have a moon shape for my sky picture, please?' Zac asked.

Mrs Robinson told him to look in the bits and pieces box. 'You might find some shiny silver paper in there,' she said. And he did.

When he had finished, Mrs Robinson made a loop at the top. 'Now you can hang this up in your bedroom window,' she told him, 'so that the light will shine through the yellow paper. It will help you to remember that God who made the light and darkness and the moon and stars is always looking after us.'

'Look what I've made,' said Zac as soon as Mum arrived at lunchtime. 'Mrs Robinson says I've got to hang it near my window,' Zac told her. 'Spidajig can sit on my toybox instead. He'll like that. Friendly monsters are good at looking after toys, aren't they?'

'I'm sure they are,' smiled Mum.

At bedtime, Mum hung up Zac's picture. As Zac lay in bed, the light from the streetlamp shone through the yellow tissue paper and made it glow brightly.

'I don't think I'll be afraid of the darkness any more,' he said to his mum, 'because God's looking after me all the time, isn't he?'

'Yes,' said Mum.

Zac looked at Spidajig who was sitting on top of the toybox.

Spidajig smiled back at him with his usual happy, rather wobbly smile.

'Goodnight Spidajig,' Zac said, and soon fell fast asleep.

Dear God
At night-time, everything looks so different. Shadows and shapes of ordinary things sometimes look scary and frightening. And, because everything is so still and quiet, even little noises sound loud or eerie. Help me to remember that you who made the day and night, light and darkness, the sun, moon and stars, are always looking after me. AMEN

Just Ted

Ted was a rather elderly, brown teddy bear who had been cuddled so much that his furry coat was rather thin in places. So he wore a green and yellow striped jumper to hide it. He wore a green bow-tie round his neck to hide the stitching where he had been mended when the stuffing had started to come out. And one ear, which had come off when Sally and Peter had had a fight over him, had not been stitched back on in exactly the right place. So he looked a little lopsided, but that did not really matter.

Ted was not called Edward or Alexander or Rupert or Paddington or any of the names people usually call their favourite teddy bears – he was just Ted.

Sally's mum had been helping at a jumble sale one day and Ted was amongst the things that were left over at the end of the sale. No one had wanted to buy him.

'Please can *I* have him?' asked Sally.

'If you like,' replied Mum, 'but I think he could do with a really good wash when we get home.'

When he was washed and his fur had been brushed and he had some new clothes, Ted looked a very handsome bear indeed, even if his furry coat was rather thin in places and one ear was lopsided. He soon became part of the family and Sally loved him very much. She took him to playgroup and church (where he always sat on his own seat next to her) and to the shops and to the dentist's (where he always had a ride in the dentist's chair) and, of course, to bed.

If Sally felt sad she sometimes cried into Ted's fur so that it became quite wet and had to be dried with the hairdrier. Or she sucked the end of Ted's bow tie until it went all soggy and horrible and it had to be washed and ironed. Sometimes, Sally whispered secrets into his ear and knew Ted would not tell anyone what she had said. Ted was her friend.

Of course, when Sally and Peter, her brother, and the rest of the family went on holiday, Ted had to go as well. He sat on Sally's knee so that she could show him lots of interesting things out of the car windows.

The first summer Ted lived with them, the family stayed in a farmhouse in the country. Sally liked seeing all the tiny yellow chickens which had just hatched and holding one gently in her hands. It felt soft and fluffy and its beak tickled her hand as it tried to peck her. She liked seeing the newly-born calves too and letting them suck her fingers.

'Let's go for a walk this afternoon,' said Dad. 'It's a lovely day and I'd like to walk through those fields and up the hill over there.'

'It's rather a long way,' said Mum. 'Sally's legs might get very tired.'

'Well if they do, I'll have to give her a piggyback,' smiled Dad.

At first, Sally ran through the fields and found lots of bright yellow buttercups, and some pieces of wool on the fence where the sheep had rubbed against it. She gave them to Mum to save for her. Sally and Peter found some sticky grass and laughed as they threw it and it stuck to Dad's shirt. They sat down and had a drink and some crisps and Sally had so much to look at and do that she forgot about being tired. Ted, who of course had come too, sat in Dad's rucksack where he had a good view of the countryside.

Then they climbed over a stile and up a steeper path and climbed higher and higher until Peter, with Sally close behind him, reached the top of the hill. From there you could see all the fields and the villages below, and the tiny stream that wove its way down the hillside into the valley. They all sat down and had a rest.

'There are some dark clouds over there,' said Dad. 'I think we'd better hurry up and get home before it rains.'

But half way down the hill, they felt some large spots of rain.

'Hurry up,' said Dad.

'I can't, my legs are tired,' said Sally.

So Dad gave the rucksack to Mum to carry and he gave Sally a piggyback to the bottom of the hill where there was a clump of trees where they could shelter. But the path was narrow and bumpy and, as they hurried down the path, no one noticed that Ted had fallen out of the rucksack and into a clump of nettles.

'Where's Ted?' asked Sally, when it was bedtime.

'In the rucksack,' said Dad.

'He isn't,' said Sally.

'Well, ask Mum where she's put him,' said Dad.

'Where's Ted?' asked Sally.

'In the rucksack,' said Mum.

14

'He isn't,' said Sally, 'so . . . SOMEBODY MUST HAVE LOST HIM!'

And Sally began to cry, but this time when she felt sad there was no teddy's fur to cry into so Dad's shirt got wet instead.

'We've got to find Ted,' she sobbed. 'Go and look for him NOW.'

'But it's dark and it's raining,' said Dad. 'We can't go now. We'll have to wait until morning.'

Sally cried and cried until she went to sleep. It was horrible being in a different house and a different bedroom, especially when Ted was not there for her to cuddle.

On the hillside, early next morning, some sheep saw something green and yellow and brown lying in the clump of nettles. They wandered over to investigate, and gently nudged it with their noses into some long grass.

'That's a funny looking rabbit,' baaed one of them.

'If it's a rabbit, it's a very wet one,' baaed the other, and decided the grass and nettles were far more interesting.

A farmer and his sheepdog arrived to make sure the sheep were all right. The dog saw the teddy bear lying on the path and went to see what it was. He sniffed at him, barked and began to toss him to and fro between his two front paws. Then he picked Ted up in his mouth and dropped him on the path. The farmer whistled and the dog knew that meant he had to go and round up the sheep. The farmer walked across and had a look at what the sheepdog had been playing with.

'Oh,' he said, 'it's just some old teddy bear. I suppose

someone must have dropped it.' And he picked Ted up and put him on the fence where he could begin to dry in the morning sunshine.

A lady came jogging along the path and saw something green and yellow and brown sitting on the fence. 'I wonder what that is,' she said to herself, and ran over to have a look.

'Oh dear,' she said, picking Ted up and knocking off some of the mud, 'I think someone must be missing you very much. I'll put you on the stile where you can be seen more easily if someone comes to look for you.'

So when Sally and Peter and their mum and dad had finished breakfast, they went to look for Ted. They looked among the buttercups and the nettles, under the trees where they had sheltered, in the field with the sheep, near the fence where they had found the wool, and by the stream that wound its way into the valley, and they walked along the path until, at last, Sally saw what she was looking for – her teddy bear. He was sitting on the stile looking very muddy and wet and his ear looked more lopsided than ever. She laughed and gave him a cuddle, even though he was wet.

'How do you know he's the right teddy?' teased Dad.

Sally laughed. 'Don't be silly, Daddy, of course he's my teddy,' she said. 'There's only one special teddy like mine.'

She carried Ted all the way home herself – just to make sure no one dropped him and lost him again – and when they got back to the farmhouse where they were staying she told the lady all about what had

happened, she said she would give him and his clothes a really good wash to get rid of all the mud. And when Ted was washed and his fur had been brushed he looked a very handsome bear indeed, even if his furry coat was a bit thin in places and one ear was lopsided. In fact, he was not 'just Ted' at all but a really special bear who was loved very much.

There are some things which are very special to us and we get very upset if we lose them. Thank you, God, that we are all very special to you and that you love us very much. AMEN

God's World

Wriggly worms and
slithering snakes;
Caterpillar looping
along a path.
Dolphins swimming;
A mouse's tail;
Water emptying
out of the bath

But . . .

What would it be like if there were no wiggles and no squiggles

and God had

made his whole

world SQUARE?

Swirling leaves and
rippling puddles;
Gentle waves lapping
upon the shore.
A furrowed field;
A camel's hump;
Snow that's drifted
against a door.

But . . .

What would it be like if there were no wiggles and no squiggles

and God had

made his whole

world SQUARE?

Bright summer sun,
soft floating clouds;
Silver moon shining
in the night sky.
Shiny conkers,
glossy berries;
Apples and pears to
make a fruit pie.

But . . .

What would it be like if there were no curves and circles

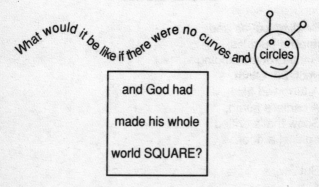

and God had

made his whole

world SQUARE?

Small green peas and
juicy melons;
Golden sunflowers
stately and tall.
Orange rosehips,
Ripe tomatoes;
Prickly hedgehog curled
up in a ball.

But . . .

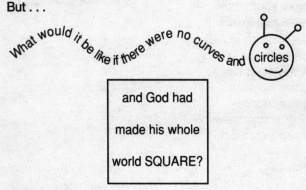

What would it be like if there were no curves and circles

and God had

made his whole

world SQUARE?

Tigers' stripes and
leopards' spots;
Blue and green markings on
a peacock's tail.
Ice on windows;
a spider's web;
Curly shell of
a slimy snail.

So . . .

Thank you, God,
for all these patterns,
wiggles and squiggles,
circles and curves.
It's a beautiful place
so thank you, God,
that you didn't
make your whole
world SQUARE!

When Dad lost his voice

Martin's dad had a very loud, deep voice. Every morning, Martin knew when Dad was in the bathroom because, above the noise of the shower, he could hear his dad singing. Martin's dad was always singing – or whistling. Granny Edwards said that was 'because he was born in Wales, see. Welsh people are very musical, you know.' But Mum said that it was because when Dad was happy he felt like singing, and if he ever felt sad, singing made him feel happy again.

Martin was not sure which of them was right but he knew his dad liked singing because he did it all the time. When he worked in the garden, digging the vegetable patch, weeding the flower beds or mowing the lawn, Dad sang. When he worked in the garage, sawing wood or servicing the car, Dad sang or whistled. He had tried to teach Martin to whistle too, but all that Martin could manage was a funny sort of whisper as he blew through his front teeth. But Dad could whistle very loudly, especially if he put two of his fingers in his mouth before he blew. When Sandy the dog heard Dad whistle she always came running back immediately, but when Martin whistled, Sandy kept on running.

'Never mind, son,' Dad would say. 'All you need is practice.'

Whenever he drove the car, Dad switched on the radio and sang along to the music. And on Sundays, Dad sang in the church choir. Paul, Martin's older brother, was also in the choir, and Martin could hardly wait until he was eight and could join the choir too. He wanted to wear a blue robe with a frilly collar and walk down the centre of the church at the end of the service just like Paul did. Sometimes, Dad sang a solo and afterwards lots of people would say 'Hasn't he got a lovely voice?' Martin was not sure about that but Granny Edwards always smiled and said, 'Yes, it's because he's Welsh, see,' and Mum told Martin that it made Dad happy to sing in church because it was his way of saying 'Thank you' to God.

Sometimes, Mum would take Martin to watch Paul playing in a football match at the Junior school. Paul was the goalkeeper in the team and Dad, because he was a teacher at the school and liked football, was the manager. Dad ran up and down the sideline of the football pitch and shouted excitedly.

'Come on, Fernwood,' he'd shout, 'let's have another goal!' And Martin would shout too.

Whenever Fernwood scored a goal, Dad clapped and cheered and shouted, 'Well done lads, let's have another one!' And Martin would clap and cheer too.

If Martin's dad was cross, he spoke loudly.

When he was very cross, he shouted.

And when he was very, very cross he shouted really loudly, but that did not happen very often. Paul said that if anyone was naughty at school everyone knew because you could hear Dad shouting down the other end of the corridor, but Dad just laughed and said, 'Don't you believe a word of it. No one in *my* class is *ever* naughty!'

Martin liked it best when Dad read him a story at bedtime. Because Dad's voice was so loud and deep he was very good at pretending to be a grumpy giant, a fierce wolf or Daddy Bear with a deep growl. Sometimes Martin felt quite frightened because he made it sound so real, but then Dad would pretend to be a princess or Red Riding Hood or Baby Bear instead and talk in a high squeaky voice. It sounded so silly that Martin and Dad would both end up laughing and Martin did not feel frightened any more.

When Martin's dad was sad, which was not very often either, he spoke very quietly and softly. So one morning, when Martin got out of bed and heard the sound of the shower but could not hear Dad singing, he was very surprised.

'Oh dear,' he thought, 'I wonder why Dad is sad.'

Then he heard a funny gurgling noise just like the one the bath water always made before it disappeared down the plug hole.

'That's funny,' he said to himself. 'Dad doesn't usually sing like that.'

At breakfast, Dad opened his mouth to ask Paul to pass him the marmalade to put on his toast and no sound came out. Paul did not hear what he said so he passed him the sugar instead. Dad started waving his arms and pointing and Paul and Martin burst out laughing because he looked so funny.

'What's the matter with Dad?' asked Martin.

'He's lost his voice,' Mum answered. 'He's got a sore throat.'

'Your class will like that,' grinned Paul. 'They can be as naughty as they like today, because you can't shout at them.'

Dad opened his mouth to tell Paul that no one in *his* class was *ever* naughty but no sound came out so he closed it again and glared at him instead.

Jack, the man who lived next door, rang the door bell.

'I've brought you a few of my potatoes and carrots,' he said. 'Fresh from my garden they are.'

'Lovely,' said Mum.

Dad opened his mouth to say 'Thank you' but no noise came out.

'Oh dear,' grinned Jack, 'been shouting at those poor children in your class again have you? Never mind, I'll bring you some of my throat sweets. They'll make you better in no time!'

Jack brought the throat sweets and watched while Dad sucked one.

'Good aren't they?' he said, and Dad tried to pretend they were although his mouth felt as if it was on fire. Martin thought they smelled horrible and was pleased that *he* did not have a sore throat.

Mum decided that a hot lemon and honey drink would be much better, but Granny Edwards soon arrived and had other ideas.

'What you need,' she said, 'is home-made vegetable soup with lots of leeks in it. Have you better in no time it will.' And off she bustled to make some.

Mum took Paul to school and Dad stayed at home.

'But what about the football match after school?' asked Paul. 'We need Dad to tell us what to do.'

'Someone else will have to look after you for once,'

she said, 'But Martin and I will come and cheer for your team.'

'Thanks,' said Paul, but it was not the same without Dad – especially when they lost the match. Paul felt miserable because he let three goals into the net. When Paul told him what had happened Dad put his arm on Paul's shoulder and Paul knew that meant 'Never mind.'

Dad went to see the doctor who shone a light into his throat.

'That's a nasty sore throat, Mr Edwards,' he said. 'Try not to talk for a few days, but then that's not very easy in your job, is it?'

'No,' mumbled Dad.

The doctor gave him a prescription to get some medicine from the chemists.

'That medicine is marvellous for sore throats,' he said. 'You should soon be much better.'

That night, Mum read a bedtime story to Martin but it was not nearly as good as when Dad read to him. Mum was better at pretending to be little Billy Goat Gruff but she was not nearly fierce enough to be the troll who lived under the bridge.

'Mum,' asked Martin when she'd finished the story, 'where does your voice go to when you lose it?'

Mum laughed. 'It doesn't really get lost,' she said, 'but when you get a sore throat it sometimes means you can't talk or sing because it hurts too much or, if you do try to talk, your voice often sounds quiet and croaky.'

'Will Dad get better soon?' asked Martin.

'I expect so,' said Mum. 'His throat should be better by next week.'

'Could we ask God to make Dad better?' asked Martin.

'Of course,' said Mum. 'God cares especially about people who are ill.'

So Martin told God about Dad losing his voice and about Paul being unhappy because he had lost the football match.

The next morning, Dad could talk in a whisper. The day after that he was a lot better and the doctor said that he could go back to work.

'I told you that medicine was good,' he said.

But . . . Jack who lived next door was sure that it was *his* throat sweets that had made Dad better. Granny Edwards was certain that it was *her* vegetable soup with lots of leeks in it which had cured him. Mum thought her hot lemon and honey drinks had helped. Martin was not sure *what* had made Dad's throat better – perhaps somehow *all* of them had helped – but he knew that when you talk to God about anything . . . he always listens.

Dear God,
Thank you that you care especially about people who are ill. Help them to remember that you understand how they feel and that you are always with them. Please help doctors and nurses to make them well again. AMEN

The Wind

I watched the ripples on the puddles in the park,
I felt the breeze blowing softly through my hair.
It felt sort of cold as it brushed against my face,
I couldn't see the wind but I knew it was there.

I heard the leaves rustle as the wind blew through
the trees.
It playfully tossed bits of paper in the air.
Branches started creaking as the treetops bent and
swayed,
I couldn't see the wind but I knew it was there.

It made enormous clouds drift across the dark sky,
It was fun to fly my kite so high in the air.
There were windsurfers speeding across the big
lake,
I couldn't see the wind but I knew it was there.

I see the colours and the patterns in God's world.
I've food to eat and a family who care.
I'm sure that he's listening when I talk to him,
I've never seen God but I know he's there.

Sam and the hole in the road

Sam Isaacs is four years old. He is always asking questions which begin with words like 'why?' 'how?' 'when?' and 'what for?'

Dad says Sam has a lively mind.

Mum says Sam is nosey.

Gran says Sam is just a normal, lively boy who likes to find out how everything works.

Sam's sister Amy is nearly two years old. Amy likes opening cupboards to find out what is inside. She sometimes turns boxes and bins upside down and empties everything onto the floor. That makes Mum very cross because *she* has to clear up the mess afterwards.

Dad says Amy is lovely.

Mum says Amy is a little horror.

Gran says Amy is just like Amy's mum used to be when *she* was nearly two.

Mrs Isaacs, Sam and Amy's mum, is a nurse. She works in a hospital and helps to look after mums and their new babies.

Mr Isaacs is a policeman. He works in a big town a few miles away from their house.

If Mr and Mrs Isaacs both have to go to work at the same time, Gran looks after Sam and Amy. She likes doing that . . . well, usually she does!

One sunny morning, Gran strapped Amy into her baby buggy and Sam, Amy and Gran all went down the road towards the shopping centre. As they turned the corner into the main road, Sam saw a big lorry and some workmen and, of course, he wanted to know what was happening.

'Gran, look!' he said. 'What are those men doing? What are those tools for? What does that sign say? What are those orange and white things?'

'Just a minute,' laughed Gran. 'I can only answer one question at a time, you know. I'm not a supergran.'

Sam grinned. Dad often told him that he talked too much, but if you don't ask lots of questions that begin with words like 'why?' 'how?' 'when?' and 'what for?', how do you ever find out what is happening?

'I think,' said Gran, 'those men are going to dig up part of the road and put in new gas pipes. Look, there's a big pile of yellow pipes in that lorry. Would you like to watch for a few minutes and see what happens?'

'Yes please,' said Sam.

Sam saw the men lift some metal signs onto the road. On each there was a picture of a man digging with a spade.

'That's a good picture,' said Sam. 'I wish I could draw like that.'

The workmen put a row of orange and white cones on the road.

'What are those for? asked Sam.

'To warn the drivers of cars and buses to keep away from the part of the road where the workmen are digging,' said Gran.

'Why?' asked Sam.

'Why do you think?' said Gran.

'Because they might fall into the hole?' suggested Sam.

'Exactly,' said Gran.

One man began to swing a pick to break up the surface of the road. Sam thought that he would like to do that job when he was bigger and stronger. Another man began to use a pneumatic drill. Chugger-chugger-chugger-chugger-chugger it went, very loudly. Sam thought that was even better. But Amy did not like the noise at all. She put her hands over her ears. Gran said *she* was beginning to get a headache too.

'We'd better go,' she said, but Sam could not hear what she was saying because Amy was crying and the drill was making such a noise. So Gran took hold of his arm and began to push the buggy with Amy in it, still sobbing loudly, towards the shops.

Sam wanted to have a ride in the model helicopter outside the supermarket, but Gran said that he would have to wait until later because she did not have 20p to make it work. She sat Amy on the seat in the shopping trolley and Sam helped Gran to find the things they needed. They bought rice, chicken drumsticks, lots of vegetables, a loaf of bread, four yogurts and a packet of strawberry jelly, then they went to choose some drinks. There were so many different kinds that Sam found it very hard to choose his favourite. It took him so long to decide that Gran went to help him. Lots of people smiled as they went past and Gran smiled back.

At long last, Sam chose a bottle of orange and pineapple drink and went to put it in the trolley. Then he saw that Amy had managed to reach a pot of yogurt and was having a lovely time. There was yogurt on her

fingers, in her hair, all around her mouth and on her dress.

'Gran, Amy's been naughty,' said Sam.

'Oh no,' moaned Gran, 'what a mess!'

'Bless her,' said the lady at the checkout till. 'Isn't she lovely?'

'Sometimes,' sighed Gran.

Gran paid for the food and tried to clean Amy up with some tissues.

'I'll bath you when we get home,' she told her.

'What about my ride?' asked Sam.

'Oh, not now,' said Gran who was beginning to feel rather embarrassed because people were looking at Amy and trying very hard not to laugh.

On the way home, Sam wanted to see what was happening at the roadworks so he ran on ahead.

'Be careful,' called Gran. 'Stay on the pavement.'

'Yes,' said Sam.

'Don't fall in the hole.' said Gran.

'No,' said Sam.

He stood and watched what the men were doing. The hole in the road was now much bigger and he could see lots of pipes underneath the road. Sam thought it looked really interesting and wanted to stay longer, but when Amy heard the noise of the pneumatic drill she started screaming.

'Spoilsport,' said Sam crossly.

'She's frightened,' said Gran. 'I tell you what, we'll go to the park for a few minutes on the way home.'

'Pardon?' shouted Sam.

'Park,' shouted Gran.

'Yippee,' yelled Sam.

'Park,' said Amy happily and stopped crying.

Amy wanted to play in the sandpit. She watched the sand trickle through her fingers and then she put some in her hair. She even put some in her mouth but she did not like the taste so she spat it out again. Gran picked her up quickly and gave her a ride on the rocking-horse instead.

Sam zoomed down the slide, swung on the bars, climbed up a ladder and slid down the fireman's pole. This was fun – almost as good as being a workman using a noisy pneumatic drill. He crawled all the way through a tunnel made from a large concrete pipe and began to walk back along the top of it. But then he lost his balance, slipped and hurt his knee.

'Come on,' said Gran, 'we'd better go home and clean you two up before Mum gets back from work.'

A white van came along the road and drove towards the roadworks. It had an orange light and a sign on top.

'What does that say?' asked Sam.

'Water,' said Gran.

'Oh,' said Sam.

When they arrived home, Gran turned the tap on to get some warm water so that she could bathe Sam's knee. 'Then,' she said to herself, 'I'll make a nice cup of tea before I give Amy a bath and start to cook lunch.'

But there was only a trickle of water from the tap and soon it stopped all together.

'Oh no,' said Gran, 'there's no water.'

'Of course there is,' said Sam. 'There's always water in the taps.'

'Not now there isn't,' said Gran.

'Why not?' asked Sam.

'I'll ask the lady next door,' said Gran. 'I shan't be a

minute.'

'The workmen broke a water pipe while they were digging up the road,' Gran told Sam. 'So there is no water for a few hours until it is mended.'

'Oh,' said Sam. 'I'm thirsty. Can I have a drink of orange and pineapple, please?'

'I'm afraid not,' said Gran.

'But we've just bought a new bottle,' said Sam. 'There's lots of it.'

'Yes,' agreed Gran, 'but it needs to be mixed with *water*, doesn't it?'

'Oh, yes,' said Sam sadly. So he had to have a drink of milk instead.

Gran could not bath Amy or wash her hair . . . because there was no water.

She could not wash Amy's dress . . . because there was no water.

She could not make a cup of tea . . . because there was no water.

Sam could not play in the paddling pool because there was no water.

He wanted to paint a picture of the man with the pneumatic drill, but there was no water to wash the paint brushes in. Sam felt cross.

They could not make the strawberry jelly either.

Gran could not cook the rice or vegetables for lunch so they had to have chips with the chicken instead, but Sam did not mind that at all.

Gran could not do the washing up and Sam could not flush the toilet.

'We need water for lots of things, don't we? said Sam.

'Yes,' said Gran. 'Do you know, some people in other countries have to get their water from wells, not taps?

When the weather is hot for a long time and there is no rain they don't have enough water.'

'That's really sad,' said Sam. 'I'm glad we don't live there.'

When Mum came home, she wanted a shower but she could not have one because there was no water. Sam told her about the workmen and the hole in the road and how he hurt his knee, and Gran told her why Amy looked a mess.

'You little horror,' laughed Mum.

Just then there was a gurgle in the pipes.

'What's that noise?' asked Sam.

'Water, I think,' said Mum and turned on the tap.

The water was quite muddy and brown at first but it soon became clear again. So Sam and Amy had their drinks and Gran and Mum had a cup of tea.

'That's better,' sighed Gran. 'What would we do without water?'

After her bath, Amy looked clean again. She curled up on Gran's knee and fell fast asleep. Dad came in. He hugged Sam and gently stroked Amy's curls.

'Isn't she lovely?' he said to Gran. 'Had a good day, have you?'

'Hmmm,' said Gran.

'Great!' said Sam.

Thank you God for water. Because it is usually there whenever we turn on a tap, we don't often think about how important it really is.

Thank you for water to drink and use for cooking; for washing clothes and dishes – and ourselves; for swimming in and splashing and paddling; for mixing paints when we want to make pictures. AMEN

Mrs McMuddle goes shopping

Matilda McMuddle was a very kind, helpful lady. But she was sometimes so busy being kind and helpful to other people that she became rather muddled and forgetful. Everybody who knew her thought that Mrs McMuddle was just the right name for her.

Mrs McMuddle lived on her own in a small bungalow with honeysuckle growing round the front door. Mr McMuddle had died a long while ago. In the bungalow next door lived an elderly man called Frederick MacPherson but he said most people called him Fred because that was much easier to say. He had only lived there for a few weeks.

One afternoon in November, when Mrs McMuddle was raking up the dead leaves in her garden, she saw Fred looking out of the window and waving to her. So Mrs McMuddle went to see what he wanted.

'Could you post this letter for me please?' he asked.

'Of course, said Mrs McMuddle. 'I'm going to the shops soon. I forgot to buy some cheese. Would you like me to do some shopping for you as well?'

'That's very kind of you,' said Fred. 'I'd like a packet of cornflakes, a bag of sugar, a jar of coffee, a loaf of brown bread, a tin of tomato soup and a light bulb please, if it's not too much trouble.'

'No trouble at all,' smiled Mrs McMuddle. She liked helping people. 'But please could you write a list for me of the things you need, so that I don't forget anything?'

So while Mrs McMuddle put away her gardening tools, Mr MacPherson got an old yellow envelope and wrote on the back of it:

> A packet of cornflakes
> a bag of sugar
> a jar of coffee
> a loaf of brown bread
> a tin of tomato soup
> a light bulb

and he gave the list – and some money – to Mrs McMuddle.

'It really is very kind of you,' he said. 'I need the new light bulb for the light outside my front door. At night time the path is dark and I'm frightened in case I fall over. You won't forget it will you?'

'Of course not,' smiled Mrs McMuddle. 'I've got your list to remind me, haven't I?' Then, because she liked being kind and helpful, she offered to take Fred's dog, Pip, with her for a walk.

'Well, if you're sure it's no trouble . . .' said Fred.

'No trouble at all,' smiled Mrs McMuddle and she fetched the dog's lead.

Mrs McMuddle and Pip walked along the road until they reached the post box. Mrs McMuddle posted the envelope into the slot and carried on walking. 'Now then,' she said to herself, 'what have I got to buy? Let me see . . . there was a packet of cornflakes, a bag of sugar, a jar of coffee, a tin of brown bread, a loaf of tomato soup...' Mrs McMuddle stopped. 'Oh dearie me, that can't be right,' she laughed. 'Whoever heard of a loaf of tomato soup?'

She put her hand in her pocket and pulled out the envelope she had tucked inside. 'That's better,' she said, 'now I can't forget what I need.'

She read the envelope. It said

> Paul Brown
> 5 Appletree Lane
> Sturton-by-Middlecombe
> Devon.

'Oh no,' sighed Mrs McMuddle, 'silly me! I've posted the wrong envelope. Now what am I going to do?'

She hurried back to post the letter in the postbox and as she walked along she tried to remember what was on the list. There was:

> A packet of cornflakes
> a bag of sugar
> a jar of coffee
> a loaf of brown bread
> a tin of tomato soup and...

Mrs McMuddle tried very hard to remember what else Fred had asked for. She knew it was important, she knew it was not anything to eat or drink, she knew it was something everybody uses... whatever could it be?

The dog stopped suddenly to sniff around a lamp post and Mrs McMuddle was so busy thinking that she almost banged her head on the concrete post. Then she remembered. Of course, Fred said he needed it to see where he was going so that he did not fall over when he walked down his front garden path in the dark. Mrs McMuddle saw a shop which sold lots of electrical things so she went inside and bought . . . a large torch.

It was a bright red torch.

'Just what he needs,' said Mrs McMuddle to herself happily. She pressed the switch but the torch did not work. That was no good at all.

'Excuse me,' she said politely to the man behind the counter, 'but this torch doesn't seem to work.'

'Of course it doesn't, Madam,' said the man. 'There aren't any batteries in it yet. Batteries cost extra.'

'Oh,' said Mrs McMuddle, 'well I'd better have some batteries too.'

The man put two batteries into the torch, pressed the switch and this time there was a bright beam of light.

'Lovely,' said Mrs McMuddle. 'Thank you very much,' and paid the man.

She walked along to the supermarket and tied Pip's lead to a post outside because dogs were not allowed inside that shop. As she walked round, pushing the trolley, Mrs McMuddle bought

> *A packet of cornflakes*
> *a bag of sugar*
> *a jar of coffee*
> *a loaf of brown bread*
> *a tin of tomato soup and . . .*
> *some cheese for her tea.*

She smiled proudly – for once she had not forgotten anything at all.

As she walked home, her shopping bag in her hand, Mrs McMuddle looked up at the sky. The sun was beginning to set and the sky was full of beautiful colours – blue, silver, orange, yellow and gold. Even the grey wispy clouds seemed to be edged with gold. They reminded Mrs McMuddle of flickering candles burning on a wintry night and then she thought . . . maybe Fred had actually asked for some candles not a torch. She knew it had something to do with light and being able to see in the dark.

'Never mind,' she thought, '*I* can always use a new torch – I'm not sure where I've put my other one.' And she went to find a shop that sold candles.

As she came out of the door, Mrs McMuddle suddenly remembered Pip, who was still tied to the post outside the supermarket. She hurried back, untied him and started to walk home again. She was beginning to feel quite tired. The sky was now getting dark and the cars and buses driving along the road all had their lights on. Mrs McMuddle was pleased that the bright lights in the shop windows and the street lamps lit up the pavement so that she could walk home safely. She walked past a newsagent's shop and stopped to buy a box of matches. After all, the candles would be no use at all if Fred did not have any matches. As she looked up at the sky, the moon and a few tiny stars were just beginning to appear.

Mrs McMuddle hurried home, opened the gate and started to walk down the path to Fred's bungalow. 'This path is rather dangerous in the dark,' said Mrs McMuddle. 'If I'm not careful I could easily fall. I must tell Fred that he ought to mend the light outside his front door . . .' and suddenly she remembered that that was exactly what he had asked for – a new light bulb for the lamp.

Mrs McMuddle felt very, very silly. But it was too late now – all the shops would be closed. Pip barked and Fred opened the door. 'I thought you'd got lost, he said. 'Come in.'

Mrs McMuddle stared. 'Why are you sitting in the dark?' she asked.

'There's a power cut,' he answered. 'Look, there are no lights in any of the houses on this side of the road. You won't have any electricity either.'

Because there was no electricity . . . none of the lights worked.

Neither did the radio or the television.

Neither did the toaster and the electric kettle.

The fridge had stopped working too.

'Oh dearie me,' said Mrs McMuddle, 'what a nuisance.'

Then she had an idea. She took the torch out of her bag and switched it on. She took out the candles and Fred searched for some candlesticks to put them in. Mrs McMuddle found the box of matches and lit the candles. Then she opened the curtains and let the moon shine in too.

'It's a good job the moon and stars don't need electricity or batteries to make them work,' laughed Fred.

Soon there was enough light to see by as they grilled cheese on toast and heated the tin of tomato soup in a saucepan on the gas stove.

'What a clever lady you are,' said Fred. 'Fancy having all those things in your bag just when we needed them!'

When Mrs McMuddle told him what had really happened, Fred laughed and laughed. He thought it was the funniest thing he had heard for a long time. And he did not think Mrs McMuddle was silly at all . . . he thought she was a very kind, helpful lady who was sometimes so busy helping other people that she

became rather forgetful. They sat and talked and laughed until the electricity came on again. Then they blew out the candles, filled the kettle and made two cups of coffee.

After that, Fred McPherson and Mrs McMuddle often walked down to the shops together, but Fred always carried Mrs McMuddle's shopping list until they had passed the post box – just in case she should ever be forgetful again and post it with the letters. She made him laugh and he stopped feeling so lonely. So no one was at all surprised when Fred asked Matilda to marry him.

All their family and friends came to the wedding. Matilda bought a new dress and a big flowery hat. She made a big cake and put lots of yellow candles on the top instead of silver bells and horse shoes because Fred said he wanted it to look bright and cheerful.

They were very happy and, now that Fred was there to remind her about things, Matilda was not nearly so muddled and forgetful. And, as her name was no longer Mrs McMuddle, that was probably a very good thing!

Thank you, God, for electricity. We can't see it but we know that it makes lots of things work. It gives us light so that we can see where we are going at night-time and can walk around safely; it makes televisions and toasters and fridges work and often people use it for heating their houses and cooking food. It is very important but it can also be dangerous – please help us to use electricity properly. AMEN

What a nuisance!

It was a beautiful sunny day. Sophie the speckled frog sat on a large lily pad in the middle of the pond, enjoying the sunshine, watching the flies fly by and thinking about all the interesting things she could do later.

She watched her tadpoles swimming about in the pond and smiled. They were four weeks old now and growing fast.

'Well, they seem happy enough,' she thought, 'so I'll go for a stroll in the strawberry patch and see what I can find to eat.'

Sophie liked eating strawberries and the leaves were big enough to hide her from the view of any large birds or animals who might like a frog to eat for breakfast, lunch, dinner, tea – or even as a tasty in-between meals sort of snack.

She stretched her long back legs and leapt off the lily pad onto the lawn. Then she quickly hopped across the grass and into the strawberry patch. There were lots of big, juicy, red strawberries which were ripe and just waiting to be eaten.

'Yummy!' thought Sophie, 'they look delicious.'

She was just opening her mouth and putting out her tongue to eat the first strawberry when it happened.

'HIC,' went Sophie, and she shot high into the air, completely missing the strawberry she wanted to eat.

Sophie had got hiccups and nothing would stop them. She tried sucking some dew from a leaf but that did not help much.

'I know,' she said to herself. 'I think you're supposed to drink water upside down if you want to stop hiccups.'

So she flipped herself over and tried to drink some more drops of dew. But it was not easy and it did not help at all.

'HIC,' went Sophie again and catapulted high into the air before landing on the ground with a big thud.

'Ouch!' said Sophie, who now not only had hiccups but a headache as well because she had banged her head when she landed.

'This isn't much fun,' she thought as she sat and rested for a moment. 'Hiccups are a real nuisance. I don't like them at all.'

She spied a greenfly crawling along a nearby leaf. 'That looks like a tasty snack,' Sophie said to herself, and she quickly stuck out her long tongue to catch it. But then it happened again.

'HIC,' went Sophie loudly, and the frightened greenfly escaped as Sophie hurtled past him into the air and then landed on the ground again with one of her long back legs in a giant, rather over ripe strawberry.

'What a nuisance,' muttered Sophie. 'I've missed again. Why is everything going wrong for me today?'

She hopped off, making rather a squelchy noise, across the lawn and had a quick swim in the pond to wash off the rest of the strawberry which was sticking to her leg.

'That's better,' she thought as she rested afterwards on the lily pad. She saw a large fly hovering over the water.

'Ah, lunch at last,' croaked Sophie. She prepared to jump. 'Ready steady, HIC,' she went.

Up went Sophie into the air again and missed the fly completely. She felt hungry and miserable. Hiccups were a real nuisance. Why did she have to have them?

Every time Sophie went HIC she hurtled off the lily pad and landed in the water. The tadpoles looked rather startled and hid among the pondweed for safety. Whatever was their mother doing? The goldfish just giggled, and poor Sophie the speckled frog felt very, very silly.

The animals in the garden decided that, because it was such a beautiful summer's day, they would organise a sports day with special watersports competitions for the creatures who lived in the pond. Sophie heard about it and thought it sounded great fun.

The water boatmen skimmed across the surface of the pond as they practised for their race; the goldfish practised for the obstacle race by swimming in and out of the reeds, round the plant pots at the edge of the pond, and underneath the waterlilies. Even the tiny tadpoles were entering for the beginners' swimming race.

'But what chance have I got with these silly hiccups?' thought Sophie. 'I'd better just sit and watch.'

'Hello Sophie,' said a very deep voice. It was Basil the bullfrog. 'Are you going in for the high jump competition? I am.'

'I don't think so,' replied Sophie miserably. 'I've got HIC . . . cups.'

Basil chuckled. He thought it was very funny. 'Well, you wouldn't have beaten me anyway,' he said. 'I'm the best high jumper this side of the Thames.'

'What a show-off!' thought Sophie as he hopped away.

Thelma the toad arrived. 'Are you going in for the high jump competition this afternoon?' she asked. 'I am.'

'I don't HIC think so,' Sophie said as she hurtled past Thelma into the air and down again with a bump. 'I can't do anything right today.'

'But there are two hours before the competition,' Thelma told her. 'That's lots of time for the hiccups to disappear. I'll help you.'

Thelma hopped into the garden shed and knocked over a pile of plant pots with a loud clatter.

'Aaargh,' croaked Sophie. 'Don't do that. You scared me.'

'I meant to,' replied Thelma. 'My mother always told me that frightening someone suddenly would get rid of their hiccups.'

'Well it HIC hasn't worked, has it?' said Sophie.

'Give me a minute and I'll think of something else,' said Thelma.

So Sophie stood on her head, she drank rainwater and pondwater and dewdrops, and she took deep breaths until she thought she was going to burst . . . but nothing worked.

When the high jump competition began, she was still trying not to hiccup. The grasshoppers thought it was so funny, they could not jump as high as usual because they were laughing so much. Basil the bullfrog had eaten a rather large lunch and could only manage to

jump five centimetres. Thelma jumped five but could not jump ten centimetres. Then it was Sophie's last turn.

'Come on,' croaked Thelma. 'You can do it.'

Sophie took a deep breath and hopped towards the jump, which was actually a piece of string tied to two garden canes. Just as she got ready to jump, it happened. With an absolutely enormous HIC Sophie shot into the air, over the line, over the flower bed and into the strawberry patch.

'The champion jumper this year is Sophie the speckled frog,' she heard a faint voice say in the distance, 'with a record jump of fifteen centimetres'. Everybody cheered loudly. 'Would she like to come and collect her prize?'

'In a minute,' thought Sophie as she nibbled her way through one juicy bright red strawberry, then another and another. She took a deep breath. Her hiccups had disappeared completely.

'Maybe,' she said to herself, 'nuisance things like hiccups can sometimes turn out to be rather useful in the end.'

Sophie swallowed the last mouthful of strawberry and hopped proudly back to collect her prize.

Dear God,
Sometimes things happen to me that I do not like very much. Things like having chicken pox or mumps, going into hospital or going to places where I don't really want to go.

Thank you that whatever happens to me, or wherever I go, you are always there with me. And thank you that some things which seem bad or a nuisance when they happen, turn out really well in the end. AMEN

When we are three or four or five, we sometimes think about all the clever things we will be able to do when we are a bit bigger or older – things like going to school for the first time, or joining Rainbows or Beavers. If we've got older brothers or sisters, we sometimes think it would be good to do all the clever and important things they are allowed to do, and we're not. When we're six, we think, we will be big at last and life will be great fun – but there are lots of fun things we can enjoy doing when we are three or four or five. And, however old we are, God loves us.

The Circus

With a hop and a skip
and a forward flip,
the acrobats come tumbling in.
With a somersault here
and a cartwheel there,
they do all kinds of tricks,
They do the clever things I'll do
when I reach the age of six.

They swing on a trapeze
and balance with ease
as they walk across the high wire.
With a double twist here
and a back flip there
they do all kinds of tricks.
They do the daring things I'll do
when I reach the age of six.

With a bounce and a jump
and a bang and a bump
the clowns come into the ring.
With a soggy sponge here
and a loud laugh there
they play all kinds of tricks.
They do the naughty things I'll do
when I reach the age of six.

With a push and a glide
I go down the slide
and climb up the climbing frame.
With a slight wobble here
and a wriggle there
I do all kinds of tricks.
There are lots of fun things I can do
before I *am* the age of six.

Shussh!

Michael was a very normal, lively, four year-old boy.

He found it very difficult to be quiet.

He found it very difficult to sit or stand still.

In fact, he liked it best when he could make lots of noise and climb, jump or run.

One Saturday afternoon, after lunch, his baby sister was asleep in her pram in the garden. Michael was riding round on his new bike, ringing the bell. Then, because he felt happy, he started to sing . . . loudly.

'Shussh,' said Mum. 'You'll wake the baby.'

But Michael took no notice and carried on ringing the bicycle bell, and singing at the top of his voice.

The baby woke up. Then she howled because loud noises frightened her.

Mum rushed out. 'Go inside, Michael,' she said crossly. 'Now look what you've done.'

Michael rummaged through the toy box and found his trumpet. He started to play it . . . loudly. Then the telephone rang.

Mum put her hand over one ear to shut out the noise, but she was not sure whether Michael's Great Aunt Elizabeth was asking if she could come and see them on Sunday or Monday, because both words sound alike when you have got a trumpet being played loudly in your ear.

'Shussh,' said Mum. 'I can't hear properly.'

But Michael took no notice and carried on playing his trumpet.

'Go away,' said Mum.

'Well really, how very rude!' said Great Aunt Elizabeth who thought Mum was talking to her, and she put down the phone.

'Oh dear, now look what you've done,' said Mum. 'Why can't you learn to be quiet when you're asked?'

Michael went into the dining room. Grandad was sitting reading a newspaper.

'Hello, Trouble,' he said.

Michael began to play his drum . . . loudly.

'Shussh,' said Grandad. 'It's difficult to understand what you're reading when someone is making a lot of noise.'

But Michael took no notice.

Grandad sighed. 'There's no peace anywhere with you around, is there?' he said. 'I tell you what, you leave me in peace for ten minutes and then I'll take you down the river, fishing.'

'Yippee!' said Michael and went into the lounge.

His big brother, James was watching a special football match on television. Michael began to play with his toy cars.

First he played with his racing cars and zoomed them round the room. 'Brrmm . . . Brrmm,' he went as loudly as he could.

'Shussh,' said James, who was getting very annoyed.

But Michael took no notice and began to play with his police car and ambulance and fire engine. And of course, he made all the siren noises as well because Michael was very good at imitating the different noises cars and things like that make.

'SHUSSH,' shouted James, and he was so busy shouting at Michael that he only just heard the cheering when his favourite team scored a goal. But he was too late to see it.

'Now look what you've done,' he said. 'You spoil everything, you do. You're too noisy.'

By this time, because of all the noise and crying and shouting, Mum had got a headache and so she was very pleased when Grandad took Michael down to the river, fishing.

They sat on the river bank but there did not seem to be any fish so they ate some sandwiches and waited. Michael decided that he did not want to eat the crusts on his, so he threw them into the water instead. Soon some bubbles appeared in the water and Grandad's fishing rod started to bend.

'Look,' said Michael, 'fish.'

'Shussh,' said Grandad. 'You'll scare them away.'

But Michael took no notice. He jumped up and down with excitement.

'Yippee!' he shouted. 'We've caught a fish! We've caught a fish!'

But the fish were frightened by the noise and managed to swim away.

'Now look what you've done,' said Grandad. 'You'll

never make a good fisherman, lad, if you're always noisy!'

On the next Saturday, Grandad, Mum, James, Michael and their baby sister went to a country park where there were usually lots of squirrels. They took a bag of nuts to feed them with.

'Look,' said Mum, 'there's one. It's just scampered up that tree.'

Sure enough, Michael could just see its fluffy tail as it disappeared amongst the branches at the top of the tree. James lay down on the ground and put a nut on his outstretched hand. Michael giggled. 'You do look funny,' he said. 'What are you doing?'

'Shussh,' said James. 'I'm waiting for a squirrel to come and eat the nut from my hand.'

'Can I do that, too?' asked Michael.

'You can try,' said Grandad, 'but you have to be quiet and keep very still.'

'He'll never manage it,' muttered James. 'He's *far* too noisy!'

But Michael wanted to see and feed a squirrel so badly that, for once in his life, he managed to stay very quiet and very still. One squirrel sniffed at James' hand and took the nut in its front paws, then it ran a little way away and sat eating it. Michael watched the squirrel and thought how beautiful it was with its smooth fur, bushy tail, and dark, shiny eyes.

'Here you are,' whispered James. 'There's another squirrel coming towards you. Hold out your hand so that it can see the nut. I'll show you what to do.'

Michael was very excited as the squirrel came closer and closer. His hand tickled as the squirrel began to take the nut, and he found it hard not to laugh. But just then, some boys rode past on bikes. They had radios which were playing some loud music. A dog barked, and Michael's baby sister began to cry because the noises had frightened her.

'Shussh,' said Michael. 'Don't do that. You'll frighten the squirrel.'

But the boys just laughed and took no notice, the dog ran around barking and chasing its tail . . . and the squirrel ran away.

'Now look what you've done,' said Michael, and *he* began to cry as well. Mum held the baby in one arm and gave him a cuddle with her other arm, but it did not help very much.

'It's not fair,' said Michael. 'Why weren't those boys quiet when I asked them to be?'

'Maybe it was because they didn't understand that it was very important to you,' said Grandad.

'Of course they did,' said Michael. 'They were just being horrible.'

'Come here,' smiled Grandad. 'Do you remember the time last week when I asked you to be quiet because I wanted to read the paper and you wanted to bang your drum? And what about when I asked you to be quiet when we thought we'd caught a fish? Were you quiet because it was important to me?'

'Ummmm, no,' said Michael. 'But that was different.'

'Was it?' said Mum.

'They've spoilt everything now, haven't they?' asked Michael.

'I don't thing so,' said Grandad. 'It just seems like that. I think it would be a good idea if we go away now and buy an ice cream. We could go and look at the rest of the park and come back here later when lots of people have gone home. It will be quieter then and I'm sure the squirrels will come back.'

They went to the ice cream van and bought some delicious ice cream cones with chocolate flakes in them. Even Michael's baby sister had a lick of ice cream and got it all round her mouth.

Suddenly Michael laughed. 'Shussh,' he said, pointing to the bushes behind the ice cream van. 'Look at that. Isn't it clever?'

And there was another squirrel. In its paws was a cone which someone had dropped, and the squirrel was hungrily licking all the ice cream that was left.

Grandad undid his camera. 'If you can stay still and be quiet for one minute, I'll take some photos for you,' he said. 'Can you do that?'

'Of course,' grinned Michael. When it was really important, he could be quiet and still for as long as he liked – just like any other normal, lively, four year-old boy.

Thank you, God, for noise. Thank you that I can shout and sing, jump about, laugh, and play instruments. I don't find it quite so easy to be quiet or to sit still, but sometimes that's important too, especially to other people. Please help me to think about what they need as well as what I want. AMEN

Scallywag gets jealous

Scallywag the ginger and white cat was a very handsome cat – and he knew it!

He lived in a big old house with lots of rooms and two staircases that he could run up and down. Scallywag was not really supposed to go into the bedrooms, but sometimes when he went upstairs he would find a door open. Then he would creep quietly inside, curl up on a comfortable bed, purr contentedly, and fall asleep. Unless, of course, Mum came upstairs and found him.

'You naughty cat,' she would say, waving her arms in the air. 'You know you shouldn't be here. Go downstairs at once.' And when Mum got cross, not even Scallywag dared to argue.

But everyone else in the house made a big fuss of Scallywag. They picked him up, they stroked him and brushed his long, silky coat until it gleamed. And Scallywag purred contentedly on their knees as they watched TV and he thought, 'This is the life for me!'

Scallywag liked wandering round the large garden, too. There were lots of trees for him to sharpen his claws on, and places where he could hide and look out for birds and mice without being seen. There was even

61

a fishpond but someone had put net over that to stop him going fishing.

Some people are real spoilsports, thought Scallywag. All I want to do is play with the fish. I wouldn't eat them.

The best place to go was behind the wooden shed or, if the door was unlocked, inside it. Sometimes mice were hiding in there, and Scallywag could play at chasing them as they ran behind all the flower pots and garden tools. That was fun. If he managed to catch one, he would take it and leave it on the doorstep as a present for Mum. The strange thing was that she never said, 'Thank you,' or 'Aren't you a clever cat?' (which was what Scallywag wanted her to say). Instead she screamed and got Dad to bury it in the garden.

Scallywag liked being the boss. He walked proudly round and round the garden and, if another cat dared to jump over the wall into his garden or, worse still, tried to chase his mice, then Scallywag would arch his back, hiss loudly and persuade it to leave. Except for Mimi, the rather special white cat who lived on the next road. She was a very attractive lady cat and Scallywag was always pleased to see her.

One afternoon, Scallywag went into the hall. He was just about to run upstairs when he noticed a big box on the floor. He twitched his whiskers. Something smelled very interesting. What was it? Mice? Rats? Scallywag was not quite sure. He could hear something scratching, so he knew whatever it was inside was alive. He put his front paw on the corner of the box and clawed at it, but the box did not open. So he tried to peer through the small holes instead.

Just then, Kirsty and Anna came through the door carrying some more boxes, but these were round and made of plastic. There were some tubes and tunnels inside them and even a wheel. 'I wonder what they're for?' thought Scallywag.

Kirsty saw him scratching at the cardboard box. 'Go away, Scallywag,' she yelled.

Scallywag stopped and looked at her. Was this any way to talk to your favourite cat? Oh well, he knew Anna would be pleased to see him. He rubbed his body against Anna's leg, expecting her to pick him up or at least stroke him. But not this time.

'Go away, you stupid cat,' she said crossly. 'Can't you see we're busy? If you don't move I'll fall over you.'

Scallywag was upset. Scallywag was annoyed. What was in the box that was so special? He was the most important animal in this house and no one was going to take his place. He arched his back, gave the girls a haughty look and ran upstairs.

'What I need now,' he said to himself, 'is a good long sleep, curled up on a comfortable bed.'

Everyone sat down to tea and no one noticed that Scallywag was not in his basket. They were too busy talking about the hamsters that Kirsty had promised to look after for the school half-term holiday.

After tea, the hamsters had woken up from their daytime sleep and Kirsty and Anna sat on the sofa watching children's programmes on TV. And each of them was holding a hamster and stroking it.

Scallywag came downstairs after his nap, quickly ate his tea from his bowl and went to find the twins. He jumped on to the sofa and tried to climb onto Anna's knee. 'Get off, Scallywag,' she said. 'You'll frighten Bubble.'

'And who is Bubble?' miaowed Scallywag.

He looked at the mouse-like animal in Anna's hand. Well, there was an easy way to get rid of Bubble, wasn't there?

He tried to climb onto Kirsty's lap but she wasn't interested either.

'MUM!' she shouted, 'Scallywag's trying to get hold of Squeak.'

And Mum walked in and sent Scallywag out to the kitchen.

Poor Scallywag. Nobody wanted to stroke him, and he could not sit near the warm fire because of those silly hamsters. He thought nobody wanted him any more so he lay in his basket and sulked. After a while, he crept round the door of the lounge. The hamsters were playing in their cage, scampering through tubes and tunnels and making the wheel go round. Anna and Kirsty were so busy watching the hamsters that they never noticed Scallywag.

Stupid animals, thought Scallywag. *Anyone* can crawl through tubes. I crawl through drainpipes and narrow gaps between buildings every day. What's so clever about the hamsters?

And he felt so unwanted that he ran away. He did not come home the next morning, or the next day, or the next. And everybody began to get worried.

'Do you think he's got lost?' said Anna.

'Do you think he's been run over by a car?' sobbed Kirsty.

'I don't think so,' said Dad. 'Somebody would have told us.'

'Well, where is he then?' asked Anna.

Scallywag had actually decided to go and find out where Mimi lived, and had discovered that the food there was really rather good. Mimi's owner, who adored cats and kept stroking Scallywag as she told him what a very, very handsome cat he was, did not mind him staying there while she found out where he really lived. And best of all, she did not have any hamsters.

A few days later however, Scallywag decided to go for a walk and have a look at his garden. He missed playing hide and seek with the mice in the shed. Just as he jumped over the wall he saw that Dad was doing some gardening.

'Hey, look who's here?' Dad called to Kirsty and Anna, and they came running outside to see.

'SCALLYWAG!' they shouted, 'where have you been?'

Anna bent down and stroked Scallywag. 'I've missed you,' she said.

Kirsty ran to tell Mum that Scallywag had come back, and he followed her into the kitchen. Mum opened a tin of cat food and Scallywag ate it hungrily. He slowly walked into the lounge and looked to see if the hamsters were still there. He looked behind the chairs, under the table, near the bookcase. If they were still living in his house, he was not staying. But, they were nowhere to be seen. Mum watched him.

'Do you know?' she said to Kirsty. 'I think that cat was jealous of the hamsters. Maybe that's why he ran away.'

Me, jealous? thought Scallywag. A beautiful, handsome ginger and white cat like me?

'Don't be silly, Mum,' laughed Anna. 'Nobody could ever take Scallywag's place. He's too special.'

'Anyway, we were only looking after the hamsters for the school holiday,' said Kirsty. 'It was only for a week.'

Scallywag listened and understood. He knew that it was silly to have felt so left out and jealous. If the hamsters ever came to stay again, he would try really hard to be kind. But sharing is not always an easy thing to do, even when you are an extremely handsome ginger and white cat.

Sometimes, like Scallywag, I find it hard to share. I don't always like it when other children want to play with my toys, especially when they are new or my favourite things. It's fun when my family and friends play games with me and give me cuddles because it makes me feel happy, but sometimes I get jealous when they spend time with other people instead. Please help me learn to share, even when it is not easy. AMEN

One of those days!

The alarm clock didn't go off at seven o'clock today. It went off at eight o'clock instead.

I could tell you why, but I won't.

Dad was annoyed.

'Oh no!' he said, 'that's all I need. I'm going to an important meeting today and I'm going to be late.'

He jumped out of bed and went into the bathroom – or rather, he would have done if my big sister hadn't got there first and locked the door.

'Susie,' yelled Dad, banging on the door crossly, 'what are you doing in there?'

'Having a bath and washing my hair,' she said. That always takes ages.

'Well, hurry up and get out,' he said. 'This is an EMERGENCY.'

My Dad isn't very good at getting up in the mornings, and if he ever oversleeps, he's awful. He gets grumpy and shouts even more than usual.

I think today is going to be what my mum calls '*one of those days*'!

Susie came out of the bathroom at last and began to dry her hair. Then the hairdrier stopped working. Susie was annoyed.

'Dad,' she yelled, like she always does when something goes wrong, 'I need my hairdrier mended *now*.'

'Sorry,' mumbled Dad. 'The alarm clock didn't go off until eight o'clock and I'm going to be late for work.'

'But Dad, it's an EMERGENCY,' she said.

'Too bad,' said Dad.

He rushed out of the bathroom and forgot to shut the door behind him. So, Tom, my baby brother, decided to crawl in there and explore. He's quite a clever baby for his age – he can undo bottle tops and things like that really easily.

He poured Susie's shampoo down the toilet. I pushed the handle to flush it away and lots of pink bubbles frothed over the top and onto the carpet.

I was only trying to help.

'Pretty bubbles', said Tom, and tried to pop them with his fingers. Then he squeezed stripey toothpaste in squiggly patterns down the side of the bath.

I tried to stop him so he pinched me. So, I pinched him back, he screamed, and guess which one of us got into most trouble. Exactly!

ME.

Why do I always get blamed for everything?

I've got a feeling today is going to be what my mum calls '*one of those days*'!

'You little horror,' Mum said to Tom and carried him off downstairs. 'However did you get into the bathroom?'

So I told her. 'Dad didn't shut the door properly,' I said.

Well, it was the truth, but do you know what Mum

did? Exactly! She told ME off for telling tales.

Mum shrieked. I could smell burning. Mum had left the bread toasting under the grill and now it was all black and horrible. She put the last two slices of bread under the grill to cook. So Susie had one good slice of toast and Tom dropped the other one buttered side down on the floor so no one could eat it.

I don't like burnt toast. Neither does Dad, so he decided to have cornflakes instead . . . and finished the lot! And Mum had forgotten to buy another packet.

Just my luck! Why do I always have to be the one who misses out?

Mum said if I put lots of honey on the toast, the burnt bits wouldn't taste so bad . . . but they did.

Tom pulled the cat's tail and the cat scratched him. Serves him right. But Mum didn't see what happened and Tom cried and cried and screamed and screamed until she picked him up. The cat couldn't stand the noise and disappeared through the cat flap in the kitchen door. Sensible cat. I sometimes wish I was small enough to escape through it too.

'It was Tom's fault. He pulled the cat's tail,' I said.

Why should the cat get the blame?

'Don't tell tales,' said Mum. 'Can't you see Tom's hurt?'

She reached for some cotton wool and the packet of plasters from the cupboard and knocked over a milk bottle with her elbow. The milk spilt on the work surface and dripped onto the floor. The cat should have stayed.

'AAAARGH,' said Mum.

So Dad's cross, Susie is complaining that her hair is

still wet, Mum's in a bad mood, I've been told off twice *and* had to eat burnt toast for breakfast and all because the alarm clock went off at eight o'clock instead of seven o'clock.

I could tell them *why* it did, but I don't think I will.

I know today is going to be what my mum calls '*one of those days*'.

'I've lost one of my grey socks,' shouted Dad.

'It must be somewhere upstairs,' shouted Mum. 'Look in the drawer.'

I know where it is. Tom posted it behind the radiator on the landing. I think it's probably a rather fluffy, dusty, grey sock now so I'm saying nothing in case I get told off again. Dad will just have to wear his black socks or his blue socks with spots on instead, even if they don't match his grey suit.

I don't really mind being late for school, but Mum made me hurry up. Just as we got to the corner of the road, it began to rain and I hadn't got an anorak so the rain dripped down my neck and my socks got soggy too. Worse than that, we're not allowed to play football at break time if it's raining.

This is definitely going to be what my mum calls '*one of those days*'!

It got worse.

I pushed one of the girls because she told me I was fat. Nobody calls me fat and gets away with it. She sort of accidentally-on-purpose got tripped up and fell in a puddle. It was the biggest one I could find!

And guess who got into most trouble from the

teacher?

ME, of course.

Why do I get blamed for everything?

I got told off for talking when I should have been writing a story; my best friend decided that I was now his fifth best friend not his first best friend; and the dinner lady told me off for eating chewing gum in the playground at dinner time. It wasn't even my chewing gum – it was Stephen's!

How unfair can dinner ladies be?

School dinner was awful. The girl in front of me in the queue got the last sausages and baked beans and I had to have cheese flan and salad instead. I hate salad.

Just my luck!

When I met Mum outside school at 3.30 pm she wanted to know what sort of day I'd had at school, so I told her.

It was AWFUL!

She smiled, 'Oh it was "*one of those sort of days*" was it? I thought it might have been.'

My mum's quite understanding – when she's not cross.

Mum had made some shepherd's pie which is my really favourite dinner and we had some raspberry ripple ice cream which is my really favourite pudding. Then Dad came home and said he would take me to a football match tomorrow. They're doing their best to cheer me up – maybe it's not such a bad day after all.

Tom's gone to bed early – he put Mum's favourite bubble bath down the toilet, poured baby lotion all over the towels and, when Mum tried to stop him, he pinched her. He posted Mum's new tights behind the landing radiator too so I think she must have found Dad's grey sock. The cat's still keeping out of Tom's way. Our cat's sensible.

Mum even said she was sorry for shouting at me and Dad found Tom twiddling the knobs on his alarm clock, so I suppose I don't need to tell them what happened – they guessed why the alarm went off at eight o'clock today instead of seven o'clock. My family are all right really, I suppose.

Mum says that everybody has bad days but it helps if you remember that, even if it's an awful-absolutely-everything-has-gone-wrong sort of day, God still loves you and cares about you.

Ummm . . . do you think I ought to tell them that it wasn't Tom who twiddled the knobs on the alarm clock? It was ME!

Dear God
Sometimes, lots of good things happen and I feel happy.
On other days, everything seems to go wrong and I feel sad and cross.
Whether today is a good day or a bad day, thank you that you are here sharing it with me. AMEN

Hands

Clap your hands, touch your toes,
Clean your teeth, blow your nose.
Click your fingers, stretch up high,
Say 'Hello' or wave goodbye.

Switch on the light, open a door,
Dig the garden, sweep the floor.
Bake a cake, then eat your tea,
Bounce a ball or skip with me.

Drive a car, row a boat,
Scratch an itch, fasten your coat.
Hug a teddy, stroke the cat,
Brush your hair, put on a hat.

Paint a picture, write your name,
Build a tower, play a game.
Open a parcel or a jar,
Bang a drum, play a guitar.

*It's quite easy to do the actions to this rhyme when you
can use both hands, but try doing it with one hand behind
your back. How many things can you still do?*

*Then try again with both hands behind your back, and
imagine what life must be like for disabled people who cannot
use their arms or hands at all.*

Oranges, ribbons and candles

One Saturday afternoon, Gemma and her mummy were shopping in a big supermarket. It was nearly Christmas and there were lots of bright lights and Christmas decorations everywhere. Gemma liked Christmas because there were always lots of exciting things happening – they had had a party at nursery school, the postman brought lots of cards every morning which she was allowed to help open, and her auntie and uncle and cousins were coming to stay soon. There were also lots of bumpy parcels hidden on the tops of cupboards and wardrobes in the house. Gemma wondered if any of them were the dolls' house she wanted, but she was much too small to climb up and find out.

Today, Gemma was riding on the seat in the supermarket trolley from where she could see lots of interesting things on the shelves, did not get her legs banged by other people's trolleys and, when they got to the boring parts of the shop where they sold soap powder and washing-up liquid, could not run away to explore. But she did not really mind sitting on the seat because this was a very busy, big supermarket and Gemma knew her legs would get tired if she walked all the way round it.

They bought all the usual things they needed – like cereals for breakfast, bread, cheese, fish fingers and potatoes – and then they bought some packets of cocktail sticks. Gemma's eyes lit up. They were what they had had at the Nursery party with chunks of cheese and tiny sausages on, but the children had had to be careful not to put the sharp wooden sticks right in their mouths.

'Are we having a party?' she asked her mummy excitedly.

'No,' Mummy replied.

'Well, what are you buying those wooden sticks for?' asked Gemma.

'It's a surprise,' said Mummy.

Next they bought four boxes of kitchen foil.

'That's a lot,' said Gemma. 'Are you going to do a lot of cooking?'

'Not at the moment,' replied Mummy.

'Are we going to make some Christmas decorations, like we did at nursery?' asked Gemma.

'No,' smiled Mummy.

'Then why are you buying all those boxes of foil?' asked Gemma, very puzzled.

'It's a surprise,' said Mummy.

Then they bought four reels of red ribbon, the sort they used to wrap presents.

'Is that to tie round my dolls' house?' asked Gemma.

'No, it isn't,' answered her mummy. 'And who told you that you were going to have a dolls' house for Christmas anyway?'

'Just wondered,' said Gemma. 'Anyway, I like *gold* ribbon better. Why don't we buy some gold and silver and blue ribbon as well as red? It's more interesting.'

'Maybe,' said Mummy, 'but today we have to buy red ribbon.'

'Why?' asked Gemma.

'It's a surprise,' answered Mummy.

Next, they went to the shelves where all the cooking things were, like flour and cherries and chocolate chips. Mummy chose some packets of raisins and nuts.

'But I don't like nuts,' complained Gemma. 'You know I don't. Why can't we have a chocolate cake instead?'

'But I'm not buying these to make a cake,' said Mummy.

'Oh,' replied Gemma, even more puzzled. 'Aren't you going to tell me what they're for?'

'No,' grinned her mummy. 'I've already told you – it's a surprise.'

Then they went to the shelves where all the sweets were. Gemma smiled. This was more like it. Mummy chose a very big bag of jelly sweets. Gemma could not believe her eyes. Usually she was only allowed a small bag.

'Are all those for me?' she asked hopefully.

'No,' replied Mummy. 'If you ate all those you would soon get tummy-ache, but you can choose a small packet of sweets or a bar of chocolate if you like, as you've been really good.'

'Thank you,' said Gemma and chose a packet of white chocolate drops, which she insisted on holding tightly in case they got lost amongst the other shopping.

'Right,' said Mummy, checking her list, 'I think that's the lot.'

Gemma still didn't understand. 'But, what are you

making?' she asked.

'I've told you, it's a surprise,' said Mummy.

Outside, it was just beginning to get dark. Gemma liked the way the coloured lights on the Christmas tree and in the shop windows made everything look much brighter. She liked Christmas.

When they got home, there was a big box outside the kitchen door.

'What's in that?' asked Gemma excitedly. 'Is it my dolls' house?'

'No it isn't,' grinned her mummy. 'I think they're the candles I need, and who said you were getting a dolls' house for Christmas anyway?'

Gemma looked carefully inside the box. 'How many candles are there?' she asked.

'About a hundred, I think,' answered Mummy.

'But we don't know anyone who wants a birthday cake with all those candles on it, do we?' asked Gemma. 'Granny isn't a hundred yet, is she?'

'Certainly not,' laughed Mummy.

'So whose birthday is it?' asked Gemma.

'Wait and see,' smiled Mummy.

Daddy arrived home carrying a wooden box full of oranges.

'Where do you want me to put this?' he asked. 'It's making my arms ache.'

'By the door,' said Mummy. 'I'll need to use them later when Sue comes round.'

'What are those for?' asked Gemma.

'Maybe Mummy and Auntie Sue are setting up a marmalade factory,' grinned Daddy.

He winked and Gemma knew that he must be teasing her.

'What's Mummy really going to make?' Gemma asked as she climbed on his knee for a cuddle, and offered him one of her now slightly soft and sticky chocolate drops. 'Whisper it and I promise I won't tell anyone.'

'Not even for a chocolate drop,' said Daddy. 'It's a surprise. You will just have to wait until tomorrow to find out, won't you?'

As Gemma went to bed that night, she thought about all the things they had bought and wondered what they could be for. Oranges, ribbons, wooden sticks, kitchen foil, nuts, raisins, sweets . . . and then there were all the oranges and candles. They were not for a party or decorations and Daddy had said she would find out tomorrow. Gemma stopped guessing and decided tomorrow would come more quickly if she went to sleep.

On Sunday morning, Gemma jumped out of bed and ran downstairs. There were no boxes anywhere in the kitchen or the hall. She looked in the pantry. There were no boxes there either and all the raisins and nuts and sweets had disappeared. But where had they gone to?

After dinner, Gemma and her mummy and daddy went to a special service in the village church. The church was full of people singing Christmas carols. Gemma did not know all the words so she just sang the bits she knew. She looked around her but there were so many people there that, even standing on tiptoe, it was difficult to see what was happening at the front of the church.

'Come on,' said Daddy, 'let's go and get our christ-ingles.'

Gemma was just about to say, 'What's a christingle?' when she saw a table full of oranges decorated with fruit, nuts and jelly sweets on sticks. Round the middle of each orange was a red ribbon and in the centre was a candle set in a silver star. So that was what Mummy had wanted all those things for – she had been helping to make christingles for the service.

Gemma held her orange carefully as the candle was lit, so that the wax did not drip on her hands or clothes. Everybody made a big circle round the church and the electric lights were switched off. The candle flames flickered brightly in the darkened church and Gemma thought it was beautiful.

'The christingle is to remind us that God sent Jesus to be the light of the world,' said Daddy. 'He came to make it a happier place for people to live in.'

'But what are the fruit and sweets for?' asked Gemma.

'To remind us that it is God who gives us enough food to eat,' he replied.

'Can I eat them?' asked Gemma.

'In a few minutes,' he said, 'when the service is finished. Then we can take our christingles home and we'll light them again on Christmas Day.'

'Like a birthday cake for Jesus?' asked Gemma.

'Yes,' said Daddy.

Gemma squeezed his hand. 'Here,' she said, 'I've got a Christmas present for *you*.'

'That's very nice of you,' he whispered. 'What is it?'

'Close your eyes and hold out your hand,' she told him.

Her daddy did what he was told.

'*You* can have these,' Gemma whispered, 'I don't like nuts!'

Thank you, God, for Christmas. Thank you for all the exciting things that happen then – putting up decorations and bright lights, having parties and presents. Help us always to remember that Christmas is the birthday of your son, Jesus. AMEN

Daniel's favourite colour

Daniel's favourite colour was red. You would probably have guessed that as soon as you saw him. His favourite jumper was red with a rolled collar that kept his neck warm, his anorak was red with a green lining and, when it was raining, he wore a pair of bright, shiny, red wellington boots.

One Monday morning, it was raining heavily as Daniel and his dad walked to playgroup.

'What a horrible day,' said Dad as his hair got wet and the water began to trickle down his neck.

But Daniel, snug and dry in his red anorak with a hood, did not mind the rain at all. He liked paddling in the puddles and splashing through the water with his bright, shiny, red wellington boots.

'Would you like me to paint a picture for you?' Daniel asked Dad.

'Lovely,' replied Dad. 'Make it something bright and cheerful, will you?'

'Of course,' said Daniel and went to put on a water-proof apron.

He found a big piece of paper and Miss Perkins helped him to clip it onto the easel.

So, what colour paint do you think Daniel chose first?

Blue, green, yellow, black, white, orange ...? No, red, of course.

He decided to paint a red tablecloth and then draw a vase with some flowers in it. He knew Dad would be pleased because red was such a bright, cheerful colour.

Next, Daniel carefully painted a vase – red, of course – and then he painted some large, bright red poppies and some beautiful red roses in it. He looked at the picture and was really pleased with what he had done. Then he carefully drew a D for Daniel in the corner of the picture (because he had painted over the corner where Miss Perkins had written his name) and hung his picture up to dry.

By this time, Daniel's fingers were covered in red paint, so he quickly washed them in warm, soapy water and dried his hands on a towel. And because he had not washed all the paint off properly, the towel soon had pinkish-red splodges on it as well. Daniel thought they actually made it look more interesting than it was when it was just an ordinary white and blue striped towel.

While his picture was drying, Daniel went to play on the indoor climbing equipment. He liked climbing ladders, going down the slide head first, and wriggling his body through the holes in the large square blocks.

'Time for a drink and a biscuit,' called Mrs Powell, the other lady who helped to look after the children at playgroup, and all the children rushed to sit down on the carpet.

Daniel drank his orange juice all in one gulp – painting pictures and climbing ladders had made him thirsty. Then Miss Perkins told the children a story about a fireman who drove a big red fire engine with a loud siren, and everybody started making siren noises until Miss Perkins' head ached and she had to tell them very firmly to stop.

Then it was nearly time to go home. Dad arrived and Daniel gave him a big hug.

'I've made a very special picture for you,' he told him. 'I'll just go and get it.'

'Lovely,' smiled Dad. 'It wouldn't be red, would it?'

'How did you guess?' said Daniel sadly. 'I wanted it to be a surprise.'

'Because you've got a blob of red paint on the end of your nose,' grinned Dad.

'Oh,' said Daniel. He rubbed the end of his nose with his sleeve, and went to fetch his picture.

But his picture looked completely different when it was dry. You could not really see the vase and the poppies and the beautiful roses because they were now exactly the same colour as the tablecloth Daniel had painted.

'That's a good picture,' said Peter's mum as she went past. 'I like pictures of sunsets.'

'But it's not a sunset,' said Daniel. 'It's a red tablecloth with a red vase and some poppies and roses.'

'Oh is it? Well, it's very colourful anyway,' said Peter's mum. 'I like red.'

'So do I,' said Daniel.

'That's a good picture,' said Pardeep. 'It's just like the fire engine in the story Miss Perkins told us.'

'Don't be silly,' said Daniel. 'It's not a fire engine at all. It's a picture of a red tablecloth with a red vase and some poppies and roses.'

'Oh,' said Pardeep, 'is it?'

'That's a good picture,' said Miss Perkins. 'It's a lovely bright colour.'

'What do *you* think it is?' asked Daniel.

Miss Perkins thought for a moment.

'I think it's shiny red sports car.'

'No,' said Daniel.

'A large red balloon?'

'No,' said Daniel.

'A letter box?' she said.

'No,' said Daniel.

'A bonfire,' guessed Dad.

'No,' said Daniel, rather impatiently. Why could not anyone see what he had painted?

'Aren't you going to tell us what it is?' asked Miss Perkins.

'No,' said Daniel. And he went to fetch his anorak and changed into his red wellington boots which were not quite so bright and shiny now that the muddy water from the puddles had dried on them.

Dad put Daniel's picture on the fridge door. The red picture looked good against the white door.

'Do you like it?' asked Daniel.

'Of course I do,' answered Dad. 'It's very bright and cheerful.'

'But why couldn't anyone see what I'd painted?' asked Daniel.

'Perhaps it was because you only used your favourite colour,' said Dad. 'If you use other colours as well it makes things look interesting. Red's a lovely bright colour, but think how boring it would be if, when God made the world, he had made everything red.'

Dad took Daniel into the garden. 'Have a look,' he

said. 'What colours can you see?'

Daniel looked. 'There are pink and purple, yellow, white, orange and some red flowers,' he said.

'And what about the leaves and the grass?' asked Dad.

Daniel laughed. 'Don't be silly, Dad,' he said, 'Everyone knows grass and leaves are green.'

'But are they?' asked Dad.

And when Daniel looked closely, he found out that some other leaves were green and yellow, some were red and some were silver.

So the next time he went to playgroup, Daniel decided to paint another picture to put on the fridge. The tablecloth was still painted red, the vase was mostly red, the poppies and roses were red too, but he painted some green leaves and some yellow flowers as well.

And this time no one thought it was a picture of a sunset or a fire engine, a sports car, a large red balloon or a letter box. Everyone could see it was a really beautiful picture of a vase of flowers.

Thank you, God, for all the colours in your world, and the different patterns and shapes we can see. It would be so dull and boring if you had made all the flowers the same colour and the same shape.

Thank you for the beautiful and interesting world you have made for us to enjoy. AMEN

Emma and the tambourine

Emma's mum took out the big key from her shopping bag and put it in the lock. C-R-E-A-K went the heavy wooden door as it opened and Emma and her mum went inside the church. Emma looked around. It looked so different without any people there. It was so quiet too, you could hear the birds singing in the trees outside.

'Come on,' said Emma's mum, 'let's start work. You can polish the seats if you like, while I vacuum the floor.'

She gave Emma a can of polish to spray on the seats, and a yellow duster to rub the polish into the wood. 'You'll need to rub quite hard,' she said, 'until the seats are so shiny you can see your face in them. Do you think you can manage that?'

'Of course I can,' replied Emma.

She carefully sprayed the polish on one seat and began to rub hard with the duster. Although Emma liked the lemony smell of the polish and she tried very hard to make the wood shine, her arm soon began to ache so she went off to explore the rest of the church. She crept up the steps into the pulpit and stood on tiptoe so that she could talk into the microphone. She found a small button and pressed it to see what would happen.

'Good morning everybody,' she said in a very deep voice. 'I'm the vicar.'

Her voice sounded really different as it echoed round the empty church. Emma giggled. This was much more fun than polishing seats.

'Come down at once, Emma,' said her mum crossly, and went to make sure the microphone was switched off properly. 'You should try to behave quietly when you're in church.'

'Why?' asked Emma.

'Because it's a special place where people come to worship God,' explained Mum.

'You mean God doesn't like noise?' asked Emma.

'That depends on what sort of noise it is,' said Mum.

Emma went to the part of the church where the choir sat on Sundays. 'I suppose,' she said. 'I could sing in the choir instead.'

She picked up one of the big hymn books which were on the shelf in front of her and began to sing loudly. But the hymn book was heavy and Emma dropped it on the floor. Lots of pieces of paper fluttered from the book onto the floor.

'Emma,' said her mum, 'put that book back at once. You need to be a lot bigger and able to read well before you can sing in the church choir.'

'Oh,' said Emma sadly, and went to look at the organ. She sat on the seat and twiddled a few of the knobs, but her legs were too short to reach the pedals. She thought it must be really interesting to play the organ.

She heard the church door creaking and footsteps on the stone floor. The church was so quiet without any people in it that even quiet sounds sounded loud.

'Gran!' shouted Emma and ran to meet her. She gave Gran a big hug.

'Careful,' said Gran, 'or you'll squash these flowers flat before they even get in the vases.'

'Can I come and help *you*, please?' asked Emma. 'It's *boring* helping Mum.'

Gran smiled. 'All right,' she said.

Emma helped Gran to take the drooping flowers out of the vases and onto the heap of grass cuttings outside.

'Now we've got to clean the vases and put the new flowers in them,' explained Gran. 'There's a wedding in the church tomorrow so everything needs to look good.'

Emma looked at the flowers. There were lots of different kinds but all shades of yellow and orange and some white ones too. They smelled lovely.

Emma touched the feathery fern and smooth dark green leaves which Gran had bought to put in the vases with the flowers. She wanted to find out if they were real or not. Then she noticed a roll of orange and yellow ribbon on the table.

'I could put some of that in my hair,' thought Emma. 'The ribbons are the same colour as my dress.' And she began to unroll it.

'Emma,' shrieked Gran, 'please don't touch that!' But it was too late. The ribbon was uncurled and all over the floor, round the table legs and under the chairs.

'Gran,' said Emma. 'Mum says you should talk quietly when you're in church, and you're shouting, aren't you?'

'Why don't you go outside and see Grandad?' suggested Gran. 'He's cutting the grass.'

'But don't go out of the gate,' said Mum.

'I won't,' promised Emma.

Grandad soon finished cutting the grass and began to weed the flower beds.

Emma decided to help and pulled up some plants that she saw had no flowers on them.

'NO,' said Grandad, 'not those. *They* aren't weeds.'

'But they haven't got any flowers on them, have they?' asked Emma.

'They never will have if you pull them up now!' said Grandad. 'Plants need time to grow.'

Gran came outside with a few flowers that were too small to go in the big vases. 'You can have these if you like,' she smiled. 'Take them home and put them in a vase.'

But Emma had other ideas. While Grandad drank a cup of tea, Emma walked down the path carrying the bunch of flowers. She saw some confetti on the ground near the church gate and she picked up a handful of the tiny pink and white paper shapes and threw them up in the air. Some of it landed in her hair and Emma laughed happily. It was fun pretending to be a bride.

Grandad looked up. 'Oh Emma,' he sighed, 'that confetti is dirty. It needs sweeping up. Why don't you go back inside the church and see Gran?'

It was difficult to open the heavy wooden door, but Emma managed to open it enough to squeeze through. The flowers looked beautiful, there were ribbon bows on the ends of the seats, and the church smelled of flowers and lemon polish.

*

The next Sunday, Emma and her friends were playing their instruments in the church service. Sam was playing a triangle and Paula was playing a drum. Emma was playing a tambourine. She liked the way the metal circles jangled together as she shook it. It made a lovely, happy noise.

At the end of the song, the vicar began to talk about all the people who helped in church. He talked about the people who did the cleaning ('like Mum') thought Emma; those who kept the church garden tidy ('like Grandad') thought Emma; people who arrange the flowers ('like Gran') thought Emma, and the organist and the people who sing in the church choir. 'They are all doing very important jobs,' the vicar said, 'and I'd like to say a big thank you to them.'

Emma wished she was big enough to do an important job but the hymn books were too heavy and she could not read very well yet, so she could not sing in the choir. Her legs were too short to play the organ, and her arms ached when she helped to polish the seats in church. She wondered what job she could do. Then the vicar asked Emma, Paula and Sam to stand up and he explained to everybody that music is important too, because it is a way of praising God. 'Thank you,' he said, 'for playing your instruments so well this morning.'

Emma smiled happily. If playing a tambourine was important, it did not really matter about all the jobs she could *not* do – they could wait until she was older.

Thank you, God, for all the people who help to look after our church. It would be very hard work if there was only one person to do all the jobs that need doing.

So, thank you for the people who clean and polish, and those who arrange flowers to make the church look beautiful. Thank you for the people who smile as they give out hymn books, and the people who make coffee and biscuits for everybody after the services. And thank you, God, for music.
AMEN